MARTIN LEMAN'S
CURIOUSER & CURIOUSER CATS

Accounting for a Feline Family

LONDON
VICTOR GOLLANCZ LTD
1990

1

is for

HERBERT,
A master of butlery,
My father's own father,
He polished the cutlery.
A gentleman's gentleman,
Urbane and canny –
One day at the races
He fell for my granny.

is for

HORTENSE,
The young maid he courted,
Whose mistress was strict,
So the courtship was thwarted.
Her appetite vanished,
She languished and moped
Till at breakfast one morning
They upped and eloped.

3,4 and 5

are the

Brothers who vied
To steady the ladder
For Herbert's glad bride.
Then ALBERT was Best Man
And steadied the groom,
While ARCHIBALD ushered and
SILAS spread gloom.

is for

EFFIE
Whose longings were slighted.
Her yearnings for Silas
Remained unrequited.
My great aunt, she poured
All her passions in making
The very best Bakewells –
A vain undertaking.

7

is for

AGNES,
Cantankerous gran.
No flour-puss, this sourpuss
Was nobody's fan.
Why should Effie's sister
Be shrewish and fickle?
She bottled her anger
In jams and mixed pickle.

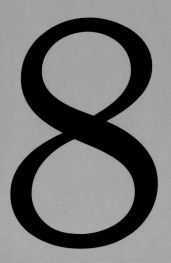

is for

WESLEY,
Agnes's spouse,
When summoned by moonlight
He'd slip from the house.
Dear grandpa, he far preferred
Mousing and ratting
To staying home helping
With Agnes's tatting.

is for

JEFFREY,
An architect who
Could design you a house
That looked ancient, though new.
In mock-Tudor mansions
And Gothic pastiches
My uncle outraged
His post-classical teachers.

10

is for

JACK,
A contemplative sort,
About fish philosophically
Casting a thought.
He'd rise before dawn
When still waters run deep
To unfathom the mystery
Of life, while men sleep.

is my

father
RICARDO, whose name
Spelled refinement in art,
So he soon brushed with fame
As a rarefied expert
On ochres and umbers
In Klee and Kandinsky –
And painting by numbers.

12 and 13

are

My mother ELAINE
and her step-brother SYDNEY,
Both vapid and vain.
Nothing gave them more pleasure
Than snow – it was wizard
To ski in a storm
And bobsleigh in a blizzard.

14 and 15

are

DONALD and GUY,
My father's twin brothers –
One agent, one spy.
No secrets were safe
From this curious pair,
Who skulked in the shadows
To poke, pry and stare.

16

is

SOPHIE,
My artistic sister,
Who lived by the sea
Where the maritime vista
And access to fish
Gave her still lifes a feeling
Of verisimilitude,
Quaint and appealing.

17 and 18

are

My kin from the Borders,
Whose mission in life
Was to take holy orders.
Politically speaking
Their difference was slight –
JAY inclined to the left,
KAY inclined to the right.

19

is

HENRY
My brother, who gambled.
A card-playing, pool-shooting
Punter, he ambled
(Like grandfather Herbert)
Along to the races,
To find a fine filly
To put through her paces.

20

is

Plenty,
Suffice to relate.
This is me you can see,
And I'm happy to state
I'm an ordinary cat
With no curious part —
If you want any more
Please return to the start.

First published in Great Britain 1990
by Victor Gollancz Ltd
14 Henrietta Street, London WC2E 8QJ

Paintings © Martin Leman 1990
Text © Victor Gollancz Ltd 1990

The right of Martin Leman to be identified as author of
the illustrations has been asserted by him in accordance
with the Copyright, Designs and Patents Act 1988.

British Library Cataloguing in Publication Data
Leman, Martin
Martin Leman's curiouser and curiouser cats.
I. Title
823.914 [J]

ISBN 0-575-04707-0

Printed in Italy by A. Mondadori Editore, Verona